For Dad

Copyright © 2015 by Carin Bramsen
All rights reserved. Published in the United States by Random House Children's Books, a division of
Random House LLC, a Penguin Random House Company, New York.
Random House and the colophon are registered trademarks of Random House LLC.
Visit us on the Web! randomhousekids.com
Educators and librarians, for a variety of teaching tools, visit us at RHTeachersLibrarians.com
Library of Congress Cataloging-in-Publication Data
Bramsen, Carin, author, illustrator.
Just a duck? / by Carin Bramsen. — First edition.
pages cm.
Summary: "Duck and Cat discover that being yourself makes for being the best of friends." —Provided by publisher.
ISBN 978-0-385-38415-5 (trade) — ISBN 978-0-375-97344-4 (lib. bdg.) — ISBN 978-0-385-38416-2 (ebook)
[1. Stories in rhyme. 2. Ducks—Fiction. 3. Animals—Infancy—Fiction. 4. Cats—Fiction. 5. Friendship—Fiction.
6. Self-acceptance—Fiction.] I. Title.
PZ8.3.B7324Ju 2015 [E]—dc23 2013047007
MANUFACTURED IN CHINA
10 9 8 7 6 5 4 3 2 1   First Edition

Just a Duck?

Carin Bramsen

Random House 🏠 New York

My good friend Duck!
Why slink like that?

Well, can't you see? I am a cat.

A cat? But you don't look like *me.*

I will when I grow up—you'll see.

My ears are still a little small. . . .

I don't see any ears at all.

You don't?

But then again,
you never know.
They might just need
some time to grow.

So I *could* be a cat?
HOORAY!
Then you and I
can play all day.

That does sound fun! Come follow me.
I'll take you to my favorite tree.

Oh, that's a pretty tree for sure.
So pretty, I could almost PURR.

Well, yes. . . .
It's best
for climbing, though.
I'll race you
to the top.
Let's go!

Oh, dear! This
really is a shame.
I think I'm off my
climbing game.

Now, now. We climb with
claws, you know.
Your claws might need some
time to grow.
Oh, yes, I think they're still
too small. . . .

I don't see any claws at all.

Well, let's find things
we both can do. . . .

Hey, there's a lake!
Let's play canoe!

No, let's play chase
around the trees

and bat at leaves upon the . . .

. . . breeze.

Don't worry, Cat.
I'll bring you back!

We cats don't like
to swim, but . . .

QuAck!

Poor drippy Cat! Are you all right?

I'll push you to the shore. Hang tight!

My friend, how do you swim like that?
Are you some kind of super-cat?

Alas, I think it's just my luck
to be no more than just a duck.

No more than just a duck, you say?
Why, you're the duck who saved my day!
You're a real hero! Don't you see
that you are just the duck for me?

Oh, Cat, you're a real hero, too!
If only I could climb like you.
But I know what we both can do . . .

. . . the drip-dry
shimmy shake for two.